UNEXPECTED DANGER!

"Let's make camp for the night," said Basil.

We began pitching our tents. . . .

I looked at the lovely woodland scene.

"It's so peaceful here," I said.

Had I known what lay ahead, I would never have uttered those words. . . .

As we pitched the last tent, Basil pointed to some objects on the ground, whispering, "We must leave! Those are undigested pellets, containing animal bones. An owl roosts in this tree—thirty-two mice would make a meal *magnifique!* And now I see another enemy—a snake! Behind the big boulder, all of you!"

BASIL AND THE
LOST COLONY

BASIL
and the Lost Colony

A Basil of Baker Street Mystery

by Eve Titus

Illustrated by Paul Galdone

AN ARCHWAY PAPERBACK
POCKET BOOKS · NEW YORK

**POCKET BOOKS, a Simon & Schuster division of
GULF & WESTERN CORPORATION
1230 Avenue of the Americas, New York, N.Y. 10020**

Copyright © 1964 by Eve Titus and Paul Galdone

Published by arrangement with McGraw-Hill Book Company
Library of Congress Catalog Card Number: 63-18707

ISBN: 0-671-41602-2

First Pocket Books printing February, 1978

10 9 8 7 6 5 4 3 2

AN ARCHWAY PAPERBACK and ARCH are trademarks
of Simon & Schuster.

Printed in the U.S.A.

For Mr. Vincent Starrett
Dean of Sherlockian Scholars

CAST OF CHARACTERS

BASIL	*an English mouse detective*
DR. DAWSON	*his friend and associate*
MRS. JUDSON	*their mousekeeper*
EDVARD HAGERUP	*a museum mouse*
THE FAVERSHAM SISTERS	*the finders of the clue*
CYRIL	*a stoolpigeon*
RELDA	*a mouse opera star*
PROFESSOR RATIGAN	*arch villain*
BIG TUPPY AND RUSSMER	*the villain's helpers*
ELMO THE GREAT	*a kindhearted St. Bernard*
THE ADORABLE SNOWMOUSE	*a shaggy mouse*

LORD ADRIAN
MAHARAJAH OF BENGISTAN
ANTOINE CHERBOU — *mouse mountaineers (alphabetically)*
TILLARY QUINN
YOUNG RICHARD
VINCENZO STARRETTI

VILLAGERS

GANGSTERS

TELLMICE

(and hundreds of other mice!)

CONTENTS

BASIL AND THE
LOST COLONY

1
Ambushed!

An arrow with strange markings was the clue that sent Basil of Baker Street scurrying off to Switzerland in search of the Lost Colony.

Some mice claim that the Sealed Mousehole Mystery best displayed Basil's genius. I beg to differ. The Case of the Lost Colony was clearly the most extraordinary exploit of this extraordinary detective.

Did it not take him to another land, to lead an expedition of thirty-two mice up a towering mountain? Was he not pursued by Professor Ratigan, sinister ruler of the mouse underworld?

And what of the shaggy mouse? Were it not for Basil, the giant creature might never have—

But I fear I am scampering ahead of my tale. . . .

It all began in London, England, on a chill April afternoon in the year 1891.

I, Dr. David Q. Dawson, sat alone before the fire. The cozy flat Basil and I shared was in the model mouse town of Holmestead, erected on a high shelf in the cellar of Baker Street, Number 221,B.

Abovestairs lived Basil's hero, Mr. Sherlock Holmes. There my friend learned all his detective lore by listening as the great man discussed his cases with his associate, Dr. Watson. It was not surprising, therefore, that Basil came to be called the Sherlock Holmes of the Mouse World.

This afternoon he prowled the streets of London, tracking Professor Ratigan's gang.

He had jailed all but the Professor and two gangsters. Suddenly I heard unsteady steps on the stair—could it be Basil? I flung the door wide—it was he!

Face scratched, clothes torn, he staggered inside.

"Ambushed! Ambushed by a starving Siamese!"

His whiskers twitched. "I turned a corner on Stilton Square, and two blue eyes met mine. A voice said, 'Basil of Baker Street, I presume?' I nodded.

" 'I've been expecting you,' said the Siamese softly.

"Then it sprang, but I sprang faster, down through a crack in the pavement. Back and forth above me moved the kitten's claw. 'This cat-and-mouse game is not for you,' I told myself. I raced along underground and climbed up on James Street.

"But the Siamese spied me! My dear doctor, have you ever seen a kitten coming toward you at a full gallop? It's a sight I would sooner forget!"

He sighed, and sank back in his chair.

"End the suspense, Basil—how did you escape?"

He winked. "I didn't. The cat ate me."

"Stop joking, Basil. What did you do?"

"Dawson, I am always prepared for emergencies. In my pocket was a packet of catnip. I tore it open, tossed it at the monster, and fled. Clearly, the cat preferred catnip to

4

mousenip, else I should not be here to tell the tale.''

His eyes narrowed to slits. ''That ambush was arranged! In all England, there is only one mouse who can bargain safely with cats, only one mouse who owns a suit of armor—the villainous Professor Ratigan!''

''Armor stolen from the British Mousmopolitan Museum,'' said I. ''It's a pity that this brilliant Ratcliffe graduate chose a life of crime. You've been trailing him and his gang for weeks, and you're exhausted. Let the police finish the job. The International Society of Mouse Mountaineers meets in Switzerland next week. Climbing an alp or two will make a new mouse of you!''

''No doubt, Dawson, but the old one will have to do. I'll not leave London until Ratigan is behind bars. Meanwhile, I shall seek relaxation. Mr. Holmes relaxes with indoor pistol practice, but I prefer the bow and arrow.''

The target was an oil painting of a horned owl. A crack shot, Basil was also a walking encyclopedia on the history of archery.

PING! An arrow whizzed past my right ear.
PING!

Another shot past my left. PING! PING!

The arrows flashed by, faster and faster. I began to feel as though *I* might turn out to be the target, instead of the owl. I feared to remain in my chair, and I feared to rise from it.

"Really, Basil! Why don't you practice outdoors, as William Tell did? Spare me! Next you'll place a grape upon my helpless head, and aim at it!"

"Splendid idea, Dawson, but it must wait."

He had put down his bow, and was peering intently out of the front window.

"A client approaches," he said. "Seems like a likely looking fellow. However, unless the case concerns the Professor, I shall decline it. Nothing must halt me in my pursuit of the ruthless Ratigan!"

2
The Mysterious Arrow

The bell clanged. Soon Mrs. Judson, our mousekeeper, rapped on the door and admitted a caller.

Basil rose to shake paws with a tall, muscular mouse.

"Good day," said the stranger. "You are Basil?"

"I am, sir. Your studies at the British Mousmopolitan must be fascinating. But do you not long for the colder climes of your native Norway?"

"I do indeed. We've never met—how did you know?"

Basil smiled. "It's unseasonably cold for April. The mice outside wear coats. You do not, yet your paws are warm. Your slight accent is Norwegian, and the envelope you hold bears the Mousmopolitan imprint."

The caller beamed. "What more did you deduce?"

"That you are Edvard Hagerup, from Tromsö, near the Arctic, an author who writes about the cat family. Your hobby is our national game of cricket."

"Amazing! Astounding! Astonishing!" cried Hagerup.

"Elementary, my dear author. I observed, I analyzed, I deduced. Dangling from your watch chain is the Award of the Golden Cheddar. In 1888 Edvard Hagerup of Tromsö won it for his fine book, *Our Feline Foes*. I perceive a pamphlet in your pocket, entitled *The Sticky Wicket in Cricket*. This tells me your hobby."

"Remarkable, Basil! And your own hobby is archery. That is why the Museum sent me to see you."

He took a sheet of paper from the envelope he held.

"Be good enough to read this aloud, Basil." The detective did so:

Dear Mice of the Mousmopolitan—

My sister and I are retired English school-
mistresses, now living in Switzerland. The
subjects we taught were botany and zoology.

We enjoy mountain climbing. One day, round-
ing a rock, we came face to face with a giant
shaggy mouse. He had a shovel-shaped tail,
long white fur, and stood <u>seven</u> inches high!

In his arms was a little lost mouse! Thrust-
ing the child at us, he fled, vanishing from
sight above the snowline. The villagers say he
often returns lost mouselings, fleeing before
he can be thanked. He is of no known species,
and they named him the Adorable Snowmouse.

In his haste he dropped an arrow, which we
enclose. Its design is unlike any we have
ever seen. Also enclosed is a sketch of the
Snowmouse, which we did from memory.

What do your scientists make of all this?

Yours most anxiously,

Flora and Fauna Faversham

Basil rubbed his chin thoughtfully. "Hmmm. May I have the arrow and the sketch, Hagerup?"

After inspecting them carefully, he said, "The Snow Lemming, or *Dicrostonyx,* lives in the Arctic. His fur turns white in winter and he grows an extra claw for shoveling snow. Mother Nature has equipped the Snowmouse in much the same way. The shovel-shaped tail is for shoveling snow, and the white fur makes him invisible to his enemies. But note the Adorable Snowmouse's low brow, the small head. The brainbox must be tiny, unlike the large brain of today's civilized mouse. In my opinion he is a throwback to primitive cave-mice, probably the last of his species!"

"Brilliant thinking!" said Hagerup. "And the arrow?"

Basil took scrapings from the shaft of the arrow, and studied them under the microscope before he spoke.

"No cavemouse made this! An arrow has four parts—the head, or pile, the body, or shaft, the nock, or notch, and the feathers, glued or tied to the shaft.

13

"Turkish mice made the finest arrows known. The short feathers show this is of Turkish design, and it is inscribed with a quaint saying in Turkish, which I translate:

THIS ARROWHEAD WILL NEVER HIT A GOOD MOUSE

Hagerup and I leaned forward, keenly interested.

"Earth and grass scrapings prove the arrow was recently used. My dating methods tell me it is a year old. Yet I know of no arrowsmith today who could duplicate its beauty. Think back to the thirteenth century, my friends! A traveling Turkish arrowsmith, Byzant by name, visited Switzerland. He married, had four sons, and joined the dwellers in William Tell's cellar. A Byzant arrow was as finely crafted as a Stradivarius violin. The Tellmice appointed him Official Arrowsmith. And this arrow—"

We could hold back no longer. "You mean—"

"Precisely. This arrow was made by a descendant of Byzant! This arrow is the clue mice have sought for six centuries! This arrow may solve the Greatest Mystery in Mouse History—THE LOST COLONY!''

3

The Detective's Decision

Deeply stirred, we stared into the fire, recalling the oft-told tale of the Tellmice.

They lived about six hundred years ago, in
William Tell's time, when Switzerland was
ruled by the cruel Gessler. The tyrant forced
Tell to shoot an arrow at an apple on top of
his young son's head. Tell's aim was true, and
his son was unhurt. He escaped Gessler's
men, and took to the hills. From there he led
the Swiss patriots in their fight for freedom.

In Tell's cellar lived a tiny tyrant, Heddmann. Aided by foreign soldier-mice, he became a dictator.

He even set his hat on a pole, as Gessler had done, and imprisoned the mice who would not bow before it.

But one day Heddmann went too far—he proclaimed a fifty percent tax on cheese! The enraged mice packed their belongings and fled to the hills.

When Switzerland won its freedom on August 2, 1291, many climbers set out to tell the Tellmice, but no one was ever able to find them.

Basil broke the silence. "Breathes there the mouse who has not longed to find the Lost Colony? I'll take the case, Hagerup. I'll question the Faversham sisters. They live in Käsedorf, where the mountaineers meet. I'll form an expedition there. And I'll leave the Professor to the policemice of London."

He paced the room. "The Tellmice of 1291 were probably helped by the Snowmice. Once I find today's Snowmouse, I'll find today's Tellmice. And I shall leave no stone unturned to accomplish this!"

"Would that I could join you!" said Hagerup. "Alas, I cannot, being engaged in highly dangerous research on my new book, *Inside Cats.*"

"No doubt it will be a mousterpiece," said Basil.

After Hagerup had gone, Basil said, "I'd like one last stab at learning Ratigan's whereabouts—I'll consult a stoolpigeon. Come along, my dear Dawson!"

We were soon down at the docks, where scores of pigeons strutted about.

Basil called to one who stood apart. "Psst! Cyril!"

The stoolpigeon sidled over. "Good day, Guv'n'r. Needin' any information?"

Basil gave him a plum pudding Mrs. Judson had made.

"I'm interested in the Professor's whereabouts."

Cyril flew off. While we waited, Basil told me the bird had once been a carrier pigeon for the Crown. Caught selling secrets to foreign birds, he'd been dismissed in disgrace and had become a stoolpigeon.

He was soon back, with surprising news—he had seen Ratigan coming out of our own cellar, at 221,B Baker Street!

" 'E gave me a message for ye, Basil. But it'll cost extra—I want your deerstalker cap!"

"Here, take it," said the detective impatiently. "I've others at home. Quickly, Cyril —the message!"

"Ratigan said, 'Tell that snoopy sleuth I stole the arrow and sketch by trickin' Mrs. Judson!' "

"Heavens!" cried Basil. "I fear for our mousekeeper's safety! We must leave at once!"

A two-horse van came by, and we hitched a ride.

I looked back at Cyril, proudly parading in Basil's deerstalker. Poor pigeon! The others snatched it from him, passing it from beak to beak until it was torn to tatters.

Mrs. Judson was safe. A messenger mouse had come for the arrow and the sketch, saying we had sent him.

"THINK!" said Basil. "Did the messenger have a high, bulging brow, and deepset eyes?"

"The very one, Mr. Basil! He spoke the King's English, and he was *so* polite, too."

"My dear mousekeeper, that messenger was none other than Professor Ratigan, my mortal enemy!"

"Gracious!" She placed her paw over her heart.

"It is well that you did not oppose him. He is cruel and ruthless. Had he nibbled your excellent cheese soufflé, you would now be cooking for crooks!"

He heaved a deep sigh. "I recall every last detail of the arrow and the sketch, but I regret that the Professor has them. I have broken up his gang. He is bent on revenge, and will do all in his power to keep me from finding the Lost Colony!''

4
Basil Goes to Prison

None of the humans aboard the Channel steamer bound for France noticed two tiny stowaways. We disembarked at Calais, and headed southward on borrowed bicycles.

Near the Swiss border we met another cyclist, Inspector Antoine Cherbou of the Paris policemice, whose sleuthing skill was second only to Basil's. He was a fellow member of the International Society of Mouse Mountaineers (henceforth referred to as the ISMM).

We lunched at noon on a grassy slope.

Cherbou gave us some creamy Brie, the queen of French cheeses. It was so delicious that I fear we stuffed ourselves.

Afterward, I lay back and admired the sky-blue sky. The Inspector worked on his weekly newspaper column, *Of Mice And Music,* and Basil unclasped his knife.

"I studied the flute in my youth," he remarked, "and shall whittle a flute from this willow wand."

"Capital!" said I. "It will be a welcome change from your vile violin-playing!"

He had finished the flute by the time we reached Käsedorf, a small mouse village cut into a cliffside.

We registered at a quaint inn, the Englischer Hof, and rested in our rooms. Then we stood on the terrace, awed by the mountains, all purple and gold in the dusk.

The Mayor himself interrupted our reverie.

"Welcome to Käsedorf! I bring a message from our Police Chief Brunner, who has jailed two British mice. He suspects they belong to Ratigan's gang, but they insist their names are Dickson and Carr."

Basil frowned. "Hmm. They must be Big Tuppy and Russmer, the only two I didn't capture. Mayor, may I spend the night in their cell, in disguise? If they let slip any information about the Professor, I might be able to snare him now, before he can cause trouble for my Lost Colony Expedition. I'll postpone the Faversham interview until tomorrow."

The Mayor agreed, and Basil went into the next room.

We scarcely recognized the plump gypsy peddler who emerged, so perfect was his disguise.

At the jail, Chief Brunner hustled Basil down a corridor. He unlocked a cell and gave my friend a push that sent him sprawling to the stone floor.

"Pig of a smuggler!" screamed Brunner, and left.

Basil told me later that he recognized his cellmates at once as Big Tuppy and Russmer. He began to brag about his smuggling gang. Impressed, they boasted of the Professor's

new gang, and invited him to join. Basil felt
he was making headway.

Then a stone sailed through the bars, with
a note wrapped around it. The robbers read it
and grinned.

"The masquerade's over, Basil of Baker
Street!" said Big Tuppy. "Ratigan's on to
you!"

"He outsmarted you," said Young Russmer. "He's at the Favershams' now, asking questions."

Tuppy clouted Russmer on the jaw. "Fool! Why did you tell him where the Professor went?"

Alarmed, Basil summoned the guard and was released.

Together we left the police station, running rapidly toward the Faversham house. My friend had not even stopped to get out of his disguise.

Would we be in time? Would the two gentle sisters tell the Professor just where they had met the Snowmouse? And what if the sisters should refuse to talk? Would the rascally Ratigan harm them?

All these questions rushed through my mind as Basil and I went hurry-scurrying down one cobblestoned street after another.

5

Missing—Flora and Fauna!

The lights were lit in the Faversham house, but no one answered our knock, and the door was ajar.

We entered upon a scene of wildest disorder! Overturned chairs and tables showed that a struggle had taken place.

"Methinks I smell a rat," said Basil, "—a rat named Ratigan! Where are Flora and Fauna Faversham?"

He wasted no time, but whipped out his magnifying lens and began examining the room, sometimes stooping, sometimes lying flat on the floor. He reminded me of a foxhound looking for a lost scent.

"Dawson! The stolen Turkish arrow!"

It was transfixed on the wall above a tall cabinet.

"Help me move this heavy cabinet," said Basil.

Together we pushed and tugged. When the wall was exposed, we saw several rows of neat printing.

Basil took out a tape measure, and applied it to the wall from floor to the top row of letters.

He nodded in satisfaction. "Mr. Holmes once said that when a man writes on a wall, his instinct leads him to write above the level of his own eyes. The mouse who wrote this began a little above his eye level, so he is about five inches tall. Ratigan fits this description, being rather tall for a mouse."

In utter bewilderment, I was staring at the message, of which I could make neither head nor tail.

I reproduce it below for the reader:

ANUA

FDNAAR

OLFD

NIFD

LUOC

SEMLO

HKCO

LRE

HSNE

VETON

"It resembles an eye chart," I remarked.

"It's no eye chart, but a cipher, or code, as it is often erroneously termed. The Professor is a mathematical wizard, so no doubt this one will be devilishly difficult to decipher."

"Looks impossible to me," said I.

"Rubbish! Nothing is impossible, if one but uses one's brain properly."

He copied the message in his notebook, and then sprawled in a chair, long legs crossed before him.

I knew better than to talk at a time like this. His brow furrowed again and again in concentration.

Then he leaped to his feet. "How stupid of me! I reacted just as the Professor expected. He knew I'd waste precious time seeking the key to a complicated cipher. Here, Dawson— read it. It's as easy as ABC!"

"Seems more like XYZ," I confessed. "You'll think me dense, but I am still in the dark."

"Why, it's elementary! This is commonly called a transposition code. Writing itself is about six thousand years old. This position code dates back to 500 B.C., when it was used by generals of the Spartan army."

"Spartan to you, but Greek to me. Basil, I give up!"

"Bah! Read it backward from the bottom."

I obeyed, but the words, as before, made no sense.

"NOTEV ENSH ERL OCKH OLMES—"

"Stop right there!" ordered the detective.

32

"The last word was OLMES, which reminds you of—"

"SHERLOCK HOLMES!"

"Precisely. The H that belongs with OLMES may be found in the preceding word. Now I shall write it down backward, breaking up the words properly."

Quickly he copied the letters, and then drew several slanting lines. The message was now clear:

NOT/EV EN/SH ERL OCK/H OLMES/
COUL D/FIN D/FLO RA/AND/F AUNA

"Then he has spirited them away," I said.

"Beast! Brute! Bully!" cried Basil angrily.

"Cur! Coward! Cad!" cried I, just as angrily.

"Rogue! Rascal! Ruffian!" cried Basil, dashing outside. "Name-calling will get us nowhere—I must find their trail at once!"

He got down on all fours and studied muddied footprints in the moonlight, then raced into the woods.

I followed. His methods were remarkable. Broken boughs, tangled bushes, twigs—all held meaning.

He pointed to a thread on a tree trunk, and smiled.

"Pink! Favored by the female of the species!"

The trees grew fewer, and the forest ended. We stood on a cliff, high above a lake.

Voices came thinly to us over the water.

"HELP! SAVE US! We cannot swim!"

Ten feet from shore was a raft, rocked by rising waves. On it sat the frightened Favershams!

Half-running, half creeping, we plunged down the face of the cliff. Wading up to our waists in the water, we reached the raft and pushed it to shore.

Basil, still disguised as a Gypsy, introduced himself.

Tearfully the sisters told how Ratigan and his gang had set them adrift, after they had refused to talk.

"But we'll talk to *you*, Basil," said Miss Flora. "We saw the Snowmouse high on Mount Emmentaler."

"He must live near the summit," added Miss Fauna.

"Mount Emmentaler!" cried Basil. "The mountain no mouse has yet conquered! The Lost Colony Expedition may be the first to reach the summit!"

"The Professor's expedition has taken practice climbs on the lower slopes," said Miss Flora. "They have even seen the Adorable Snowmouse!"

Miss Fauna nodded. "The gangsters said they set a trap for the creature, but one of their own mice was trapped instead, and the Snowmouse got away."

Basil sighed. "I haven't even had time to form my own expedition. However, it shouldn't prove difficult. The ISMM is meeting at the Englischer Hof tonight. I shall ask for volunteers."

In excellent spirits, we left the Favershams at their door, and made our way back to the inn.

6

Events at the
Englischer Hof

Basil entered our rooms as a Gypsy, but emerged as a detective, in deerstalker cap and Inverness cape.

The ISMM members had just elected a new president, Maestro Vincenzo Starretti, a musical conductor of note.

Seeing us enter, he said, "We are honored by the presence of a past president. ISMM members, I give you the Sherlock Holmes of the Mouse World!"

Everyone sat erect, awaiting Basil's words.

"Fellow summit-seekers! I am about to attempt the impossible—the discovery of the Lost Colony. I believe that today's Tellmice dwell in some hidden valley, and that the Adorable Snowmouse will lead us to them!

"In 1852 a man, the Chief Indian Computer, estimated Mount Everest's height. Last year I surveyed our own Emmentaler, by the same method, observing the summit from six different places, miles away. I measured the angles with theodolites, which are like telescopes, and averaged my figures. Roughly, Emmentaler stands 9,000 feet to Everest's 29,000. As Everest is to man, so Emmentaler is to mice—the eternal challenge! What brave mountaineers will join my expedition?"

Every mouse present raised his paw! After interviewing the best climbers, Basil signaled for silence.

"Tomorrow I'll post the names of those chosen. I wired ahead for supplies and equipment, which are already stored in the innkeeper's barn. I need a day to supervise the packing. We depart at dawn on the day following. My thanks to all of you."

After the applause, Starretti announced a surprise.

"I have conducted many operas starring the famous mouse soprano, Relda. Here on holiday, she has kindly consented to sing for us. Introducing—Relda!"

She was a little beauty—her fur was flecked with gold, as were her eyes. Her throat was golden, too.

At the piano the Maestro accompanied her admirably, never overshadowing that creamy, exquisite voice.

She gave us Brahms and Schubert, and then began the Bell Song, from the opera *Lakmé*.

As though in a trance, Basil ascended the platform, and joined in with his flute, playing flawlessly.

In the beautiful passage where voice and flute harmonize, he blended his trills so perfectly with hers that I could not tell one from the other.

As one mouse we rose, shouting, "Bravo! Bravo! BRAVISSIMO!"

She encored with the Laughing Song, from *Die Fledermaus,* and the *Well-Tempered Yodeler,* by Cherbou.

But no sooner did the last pearly echo die away than there were cries of "FIRE! FIRE!"

Calm prevailed. Visitors and villagers passed pails from paw to paw until the flames were extinguished.

Ten minutes later the innkeeper came seeking Basil.

He was greatly agitated. "Good sir! I bring bad news. While we were all fighting the fire, thieves entered my barn. Your equipment has been stolen!"

Basil sprang to his feet. "Fool that I was! I should have had the barn guarded. It takes no genius to know who masterminded this theft—Professor Ratigan!''

Outside the barn he scanned the ground. ''Alas, a certain set of tracks is all too familiar.''

I did not answer. My nose was directing me elsewhere, toward an enchanting aroma.

My legs led me on, and soon I saw what I had been sniffing—a hill of cheese as high as my knees!

Blissfully I bent over the great golden mound, my mouth watering in anticipation.

''STOP! IT'S A TRAP!''

Basil came running up. Slowly and cautiously he poked at the cheese with a long stick.

I heard the click of steel jaws, and the stick snapped in two! Concealed beneath the cheese was the deadly mechanism so dreaded by mice! We shuddered to our tailtips. One false move and—!!!

Basil said grimly, "The Professor knew we'd come. To think that a mouse would use a mousetrap against his own kind! How low can one sink?"

Back in our rooms I remarked, "He has supplies and a head start. Will there be much delay?"

"Heaven knows! Our huge order emptied the local shops. New supplies may not arrive for several days. When they do, I must see to the sorting and packing. Now I shall have to stay up all night deciding upon a basic plan of operation for the entire expedition."

And he did just that, as his tired eyes testified the next day. He posted the list of picked expeditioneers, and we went gloomily in to breakfast. I noticed the Mayor and a group approaching our table.

The Mayor's words turned our sadness to gladness!

The good mice of Käsedorf had gone from house to house, collecting every single item we needed!

"More than enough for an expedition," said the Mayor. "After all, climbing is our national sport. And many of our villagers beg to carry the loads. Your star climbers must save their strength for the heights, where every step is a mighty effort."

Basil rose. "Dear Mice of Käsedorf! You are all leagued together in kindness, and I hereby name you The Kindhearted League. I'll bring the Tellmice back, and make your little town world-famous!"

The supplies were piled in the public square —tents, boots, sleeping bags, rope ladders, stoves, clothes, medicines, and food—fresh and in tins, from cheese to chocolate bars. There was even a metal sectional ladder Basil had designed some years back.

He said we would depart at dawn, and told the expeditioneers to relax at the inn. Basil and I stayed to supervise the bearers as they packed the loads.

The ravishing Relda appeared. She said she had scaled many peaks, and that Emmentaler fascinated her.

"Basil, may I join your expedition? I won't be any trouble, and I'll do all the mending and darning."

He patted her paw. "My dear, I regret to refuse one so fair. But my mice would pay more heed to your charms than to their mission. And what if you should catch cold? For the sake of your public—stay home!"

The singer stalked off in tears.

"Mending and darning indeed!" muttered Basil. "Does she think we are off on a Sunday school picnic? This expedition is for males only!"

7

Elmo the Great

In the darkness just before dawn, we set off on our perilous journey into the unknown.

The rucksacks on our backs held climbing gear, and coils of rope were slung around us. Cheerful Swiss bearers carried the really heavy loads.

Singing Alpine songs, we trudged along narrow streets, crossed a wooden footbridge, and then took a twisting pathway upward through the woods.

We halted on the shores of a lake with

shimmering blue waters. The view was breath-taking!

Ringed around the lake was a range of mountains. On the far shore loomed the proudest peak of all—snow-capped Mount Emmentaler.

This mighty pyramid, towering skyward, was our opponent. It was dotted with cliffs

and crevasses, and great overhaning glaciers on its upper slopes.

Splashing sounds told me my companions were frolicking in the lake. I joined them. Basil was wading around, informally greeting his expeditioneers.

Tillary Quinn, who wrote crime stories as a hobby, was a New Zealander who excelled in ice-climbing.

"Tillary, you were first choice!" said Basil.

47

He waved to Starretti, Cherbou, and the Maharajah of Bengistan, superb climbers all. The Oriental ruler, once Basil's roommate at Ratcliffe, had invited us to his palace in Asia. His private zoo featured midget monkeys he himself had captured.

Lord Adrian, world explorer, had finished his swim. He stood on shore, wearing the usual red carnation.

"Basil," he said, "I should have gone home on matters pertaining to my father's estate. But I postponed it—couldn't pass up a chance like this."

Basil nodded. "Wisely decided. You are equally at home on ocean floor or mountain-top, and I appoint you Historian."

Young Richard, the American mathematician from Iowa, had already won fame for his rock-climbing.

"I appoint you Surveyor," said Basil. "By the way, do you hail from your state's capital, Des Moines?"

"From Davenport, Basil. And glad I came!"

The scientist-climbers were welcomed—Howard the Geologist, Gifford the Archeologist, and a Swiss, Wolff the Physiologist, plus Photographer Jamaldi.

Last but not least, Basil greeted the twenty Swiss mountaineers who had volunteered as bearers.

We continued the climb, crossing rushing streams, linked to one another by ropes around our waists. We climbed sheer rock walls by finding pawholds and footholds where less expert climbers might have seen none.

Along our way were scenes of startling beauty. Truly, there is nothing like mountain-climbing to impress one with the grandeurs of Nature and the littleness of mice.

Late one afternoon we stood admiring a flaming sunset. Suddenly a gigantic paw was set down on the ground beside us!

We looked up in terror, but the face of a friend beamed down upon us. It was Elmo the Great, a brave St. Bernard we had met on our last trip abroad.

"Basil," said Elmo, "I had an odd experience high on the mountain, and something is caught in my fur, something I cannot reach, near my shoulders. Will you and Dr. Dawson be good enough to remove it?''

We scrambled up the big dog's body, and soon saw the tiny thing matted in his fur—a Turkish arrow!

Once the arrow was removed, Basil questioned Elmo. The dog told us he had met a strange, mouselike animal above the snowline.

Basil's eyes gleamed. ''Tell me, Elmo— was he a shaggy mouse with white fur, about seven inches high?''

Elmo nodded. ''I barked, and was sorry I did, for the sound—and the size of me— frightened the creature terribly! He ran away,

but stumbled in the snow. I followed, thinking to help him to his feet, but he thought I meant to harm him. He got up and ran away again. Soon afterward, something dropped on my back from an overhanging ledge. A weapon, I suppose.''

''A Turkish arrow, to be exact,'' said Basil. ''You were attacked by the Adorable Snowmouse, a goodhearted sort. He restores lost little mouselings to their parents, but is too shy to stay and be thanked. You must tell us just where this encounter took place, for this entire expedition is on his trail.''

Elmo listened with interest as Basil told of our mission, and the trouble the Professor had made.

He growled. ''If ever I see the rascally Ratigan, I'll take him by the scruff of his scurvy neck and trot him off to the Käsedorf jail! Well, I'd best be going. Be sure to yodel if you should ever need my help. I roam about a lot, and this clear mountain air carries sounds for miles. *Auf Wiedersehen!*''

Great strides took him from our sight in seconds.

"Let's make camp for the night," said Basil.

We began pitching our tents. There were twelve two-mouse tents and two twelve-mouse tents.

I looked at the lovely woodland scene.

"It's so peaceful here," I said.

Had I known what lay ahead, I would never have uttered those words.

We were to have still another encounter that day, one that was far from peaceful!

8
The Snake Charmer

As we pitched the last tent, Basil pointed to some objects on the ground, whispering, "We must leave! Those are undigested pellets, containing animal bones. An owl roosts in this tree—thirty-two mice would make a meal *magnifique!* And now I see another enemy—a snake! Behind the big boulder, all of you!"

We obeyed, but Basil stayed and played his flute.

The weird Oriental melody charmed the

snake. It slithered toward him, holding its head high, swinging and swaying in a strange sort of dance.

Basil also swayed, inching backward toward the tree. The spellbound snake followed.

Slowly the sleuth took the flute from his

lips, and imitated the mating call of the Great Gray Owl!

He was a superb mimic. The leaves of the tree parted to reveal an owl. The snake snapped out of its trance, the owl pounced, and the battle was on!

The screeching and the hissing were hideous to hear!

"Thanks to your quick thinking," I told Basil, "we have been saved. Let's go while the going is good."

"Permit me to parody the great human poet Longfellow," replied Basil, and recited softly,

And the night shall be filled
with fury,
And the mice, who had
thought to stay,
Shall fold their tents like
the Arabs,
And as silently steal away.

And that was precisely what we did. A bright moon guided us to a spot far from our foes.

The cooks outdid themselves that night, and we all ate ravenously of cheese *raclette*, a Swiss delicacy.

Afterward, around the campfire, we discussed the strides made in chemistry. Dr. Wolff mentioned a Swiss researcher, Philippus Aureolus Paracelsus.

Basil nodded. "A great man! Born 1493, died 1541."

"What a name," said Young Richard. "A mile long!"

"His real one was even longer," answered Basil. "He changed it from Theophrastus Bombastus von Hohenheim to Philippus Aureolus Paracelsus!"

His face grew serious. "Recently I obtained a new substance from cheese mold. I believe it can destroy infection, and wrote a paper about it—*Memoirs On The Culture Known As Penicillin*."

"I'll tell my friend Fleming to read it," said Lord Adrian. "Medical mice run in his family."

The rat-tat-tat of rain sent us to our tents.

Thunder and lightning dampened my spirits even more.

"The weather couldn't be worse!" I complained.

"My dear doctor," said Basil. "What if it were raining cats and dogs?"

I did not deign to answer, but snuggled into my sleeping bag and started snoring.

9
Avalanche!

The next morning we arose at six, had our tea, and climbed steadily for two hours. Then we breakfasted on brown bread and cheese.

At this time Basil explained his plan of operation.

"Should I be unable to lead you, by reason of illness or accident, Tillary Quinn will serve in my stead. Now for the plan. We will climb every morning, as expeditioneers usually do. However, in the afternoons I'll assign teams to fan out in all directions to search for the

Snowmouse—no nook or cranny must be overlooked. Imagine yourselves detectives, seeking to solve the Greatest Mystery in Mouse History!''

"Hear! Hear!" we shouted enthusiastically.

We faced many dangers in the days ahead.

There were narrow gaps to be leaped across, and gaps too wide for leaping. For these we made bridges of long sticks lashed together with rope, and crawled over on paws and knees, not daring to look down.

Some rivers were too deep for wading, and too wide for bridges. We would make canoes from hollowed-out branches. Once an inquisitive fish almost upset our canoe. Basil tossed him a loaf of brown bread, which kept him busy while we paddled off.

We could not cross the River Sbrinz in any of these ways. Its treacherous current and great width made any crossing risky. Basil decided upon a detour.

"Three precious days will be lost," he told us, "but I refuse to put one mouse's life in danger. We'll follow the shoreline to Bachenreich Falls. There, where the river narrows, we will cross."

We marched on, in excellent spirits. The Swiss villagers were a friendly group, except for one shy youth who seemed to want to be alone. Generally, we were like one big, happy family.

We still searched for the Snowmouse, with no success. We knew, however, that we stood more chance of finding him above the snow-line.

The days were hot. When the river curved inland, forming a quiet pool, we would sit down in the water to cool off. We must have looked rather ridiculous.

Picture, if you will, a party of thirty-two mice in water up to their chins, holding umbrellas to shield their heads from the sun's burning rays.

Photographer Jamaldi was so amused that he took many pictures of us squatting there.

One day, backing up with his camera, he sat down on an ant hill. The angry ants bit him.

When we marched on he complained so bitterly and so often of his many bites that Starretti said, "Come, come, Jamaldi—don't you think you're making a mountain out of an ant hill?"

There were no more complaints from the photographer.

That afternoon we camped on a high rock, shaped like a table. It jutted out over the river.

Our beautiful surroundings inspired Basil, who took out his flute and played Scarlatti's *Pastorale*.

Then he played the Bell Song, from *Lakmé*. To my amazement, a voice joined the flute, high and clear in the mountain air.

Enchanted, I closed my eyes, recalling how beautifully Relda had sung this same aria at the inn.

Relda! I opened my eyes and stared at the singer. The shy Swiss youth was Relda in disguise!

Basil's startled expression showed he also knew, but he kept playing his flute.

The voice soared, higher and higher, and stopped, for the earth had made an ominous, rumbling noise.

We looked at the opposite shore of the river —a crack in the earth appeared. A stone tumbled down, and another, and another, faster and faster!

Before our horrified eyes part of the slope opposite slid downward.

Relda's high notes had started an avalanche!

10
The Return of Ratigan

Nature had shown that she could be terrible as well as beautiful. We feared for our lives, but a kind fate watched over us, for the avalanche, a small one, did not extend to our side of the river.

However, rocks and stones and chunks of earth had been piled high by the slide, and a newborn hill now reached halfway across the River Sbrinz.

Basil spoke sternly to Relda. "You joined this expedition expressly against my wishes. I presume you bribed the Swiss bearer whose place you took.''

The singer hung her head. ''I sang Brahms' Lullaby for his children, and gave them my autograph.''

''So! You are the first female ever to outwit Basil of Baker Street! Back to Käsedorf you'll go, as soon as Elmo turns up. To yodel for him now might set off another avalanche. Remember, Relda—no more singing!''

He addressed the rest of us. ''Tomorrow, when the débris has settled somewhat, we'll open my sectional ladder to its full forty-inch length, and push it over the new hill. Climbing that hill will bring us near Bachenreich Falls, the highest a mouse has ever gone.''

In the morning we carried out Basil's in-
tructions.

Lord Adrian bravely crossed first, inching
along on paws and knees, above the churning,
foaming waters.

"Onward and upward!" he shouted.
"Steady does it!"

Dividing the loads equally, the rest of us
went over, at a snail's pace. We then climbed
up the hill and down it, to the opposite shore
of the river.

I took a stroll after breakfast, and came upon a picturesque old well. Curious to see whether it had run dry, I leaned over, but lost my balance and fell in! Splashing and sputtering, I cried out for help.

Basil's head soon appeared in the opening above.

"My dear doctor," he called down. "You should have attended to the sick, and left the well alone!"

My teeth were chattering. "S-s-stop j-j-joking!"

He laughed, and lowered a rope ladder. Back at camp, where I donned dry clothing, we learned that the Maharajah had not returned from his morning walk.

"I smell a rat again—Ratigan! Follow me, Dawson!"

We hurried along toward Bachenreich Falls. The roar was deafening. A column of water tumbled from high above, like a silvery lace curtain. The drop from the narrow path was dangerous—a mouse would be swept helplessly along by the raging torrent.

Basil nosed about on the ground. "Ah!

Signs of a scuffle! And the emerald from our friend's turban, and many footprints, too many! What's this? Extraordinary! The footprints end at the Fall!''

Standing up, he peered intently at the down-rushing waters, and a strange smile played about his lips.

''Aha! The curtain is not as thick as it seems. Step where I step, Dawson, and take care—your very life may depend upon it!''

Whereupon Basil strode forward into Bachenreich Falls—and vanished before my very eyes!

''Where are you? Where are you?'' I implored.

But a mocking echo was my only answer.

11
The Fight at the Falls

Obviously, there was but one thing to do.

I stepped through the waterfall, and emerged on the other side, soaked to the fur.

I stood on a slippery ledge, barely an inch wide.

Basil waited on a path that led up a low, grassy hill. Near the top we saw a cave, with a wooden door set into the opening.

Basil put his ear to the door. "It's the Professor, Dawson—we had better eavesdrop."

I heard a gloating voice. "So! There lies the

Maharajah of Bengistan, tied with his own tail, as helpless as a babe! Yet you insist, your Highness, that Basil of Baker Street will find you. The smartest policemice of Europe have never found my secret hideout. What makes you so sure Basil will?''

Bengistan's voice rang loud and clear. ''Be-

cause, like Mr. Sherlock Holmes, he can do the impossible!''

''Bah! Basil is brainy, but by no means my mental equal. I'll hold you as hostage until he calls off his search for the Lost Colony. *I'll* be the one to find it, the hero of the hour! And when wealthy mice invite me to their homes, I'll organize the biggest crime wave of all time. Today I rule the mouse underworld—tomorrow the entire mouse world!''

"Never!" cried Bengistan. "Not while Basil roams the earth to champion the cause of law and order."

"Your faith amuses me, your Highness. Big Tuppy! Russmer! Deliver a message to Basil."

But just then we were seen, and an alarm was raised.

Panting like puppydogs, we ran down the hill and through the Fall. There my friend took his stand.

"I remain here. I propose to wrestle Ratigan, for high stakes. If I win, he must free Bengistan and stop making trouble for us. But if he wins—"

He sighed heavily. "That is the chance I must take. Neither of us has ever lost a match. He is an expert at *baritsu*, a Japanese method of wrestling. I use *nanoc*, an Eskimo method. Fetch the others, so there will be no chance of foul play. And hurry!"

I hastened to do so. Only Relda stayed behind. A wrestling match was no sight for a refined female.

We found Basil and the Professor stripped

to their waists, circling each other warily, waiting for a chance to secure a crushing hold.

It was the first time I had seen the tall, skeleton-like Professor, and the look of evil on his face repelled me. His gangsters watched silently.

The wrestlers were evenly matched. Suddenly their long arms locked them together in a terrible embrace. They teetered to and fro on the very brink of Bachenreich Falls, perilously close to the edge.

I gasped in horror. Would it be my friend's dreadful fate to perish in the swirling torrent below?

"Take care! Take care!" I shouted.

But my worst fears were realized. Ratigan went over the edge, dragging the detective with him!

Mists swam before my eyes, and I sank to my knees, shaking with sobs.

He was gone! Basil, the best friend a mouse ever had, was gone forever!

12

'Mid Snow and Ice

My suffering was of short duration, ending at the sound of a familiar voice.

"My dear doctor, pray do not mourn my passing. I assure you I am quite unharmed, thanks to Elmo, whom Relda directed here. Arriving in the nick of time, he made two neat catches—Ratigan and myself."

I looked up. Basil sat jauntily on one of the dog's front paws. He hopped off, and then the St. Bernard put the Professor down beside us.

I could see Elmo's head and shoulders. He

stood in the water, only a shallow stream to a dog his size.

I thanked him with all my heart. Young Richard and Lord Adrian went to the cave to free the Maharajah.

All the gangsters had fled.

"No matter!" said Basil. "The biggest prize will be sent back to England, to stand trial for his crimes."

Ratigan, tied with his own tail, shouted, "Bah! I'll escape! No jail on earth can hold me!"

Ignoring him, we built a chair for Relda. It had a railing and a canopy, somewhat like the howdahs humans use for riding elephants.

She rode it proudly on Elmo's back. The Professor was lashed to his collar.

Weeks later we learned of Ratigan's escape.

A boulder had come crashing down in front of Elmo. He sprang back, and his two passengers were thrown. The singer was in the tall grass, unhurt, but the criminal had vanished. No doubt the "accident" had been staged so that Ratigan could be rescued.

It was well that we did not know this until later, for we needed peace of mind for the hardships ahead.

We were above the snowline, in a world of never-ending white. The sun glared so fiercely that we wore dark glasses to guard against snow blindness.

Sometimes we would halt, spellbound by the wonders of this cold, white world. The slopes of soft snow looked like the frosting on some giant birthday cake.

Many a night, shivering on a lonely peak,

There were no signs of the Snowmouse. A few Swiss began to doubt he existed, and talked of going back.

It was Basil who rallied us during those dark hours. His will to go on in the face of overwhelming odds inspired us all. His courage was incredible!

When we came to crevasses filled with huge ice blocks, it was Basil who went ahead to see whether those blocks would bear a mouse's weight.

When we reached ice falls, Basil and Tillary risked their lives to cut steps with their ice axes, that the other expeditioneers might ascend in safety.

Climb, climb, climb! There were times when it seemed that we had spent a lifetime on the mountain.

Basil sent advance teams out daily, to leave

supplies farther up for those who would climb
next.

One day Basil and I went out as a team. We
left supplies on a ledge, and started back. It
was like a touch of home to see his deerstalker
cap, which he wore over his snow helmet and
goggles.

"Look!" he cried triumphantly. "Mouse tracks!"

The tracks were wider and deeper than any we could have made. The Snowmouse was nearby!

Back at camp the news lifted everyone's spirits, and in the morning Basil assigned two teams to find the elusive Snowmouse. By late afternoon a light snowfall had become a blizzard, and we grew uneasy, concerned for the safety of our climbers.

At last several weary figures staggered into camp, coughing and sneezing and sniffling.

They had not found the Snowmouse. Great

gusts of wind and swirling snow had forced them to seek shelter under an overhanging ledge. It had not covered them completely, and all had caught cold!

I ordered them to lie down in the warmth of the cook tent. Dr. Wolff and I dosed them with pills.

It was not our lucky day. A small snowslide cut a path through camp. With it went our largest case of cheese, now buried beneath tons of snow.

This was serious! Our rations would be sliced in half. And if we did not soon succeed in our mission, we might be so weakened by insufficient cheese that we would have to turn back.

The loss was uppermost in my mind when I fell asleep, and I had a most singular dream.

I dreamed I was in London, at a magnificent mouse ball. Trumpets blared, and twenty teacarts were trundled in, laden with cheeses from all lands.

A duke announced grandly, "Dr. David Q. Dawson will decide which of these cheeses stands supreme!"

Lovingly, I began my tasting. How fabulous the flavors, how heavenly the aromas! Gouda, Gruyere—Cheddar, Camembert, Chantelle—

A fever burned within me! I forgot everything but the bliss of gobbling those glorious cheeses!

The great hall buzzed with angry voices. "Remove the glutton! . . ." "Is he a pig or a mouse? . . ." "Shameful, shameful! . . ." "Disgraceful! . . ."

The duke tugged at my sleeve. "Doctor, Doctor!"

His voice grew louder. "Dawson, DR. DAWSON!"

I paid no heed, and he shook my shoulder, screaming, "MY DEAR DOCTOR!"

Then the scream became a whisper, Basil's whisper, and he was shaking me by the shoulder.

"My dear doctor, there is a midnight prowler about—none other than the Adorable Snowmouse!"

13

The Adorable
Snowmouse

As he spoke, Basil slung his rucksack over his shoulder. I reached for mine, and did not forget my little black bag.

Running swiftly ahead in the moonlight we saw the Adorable Snowmouse. We took up the chase.

The Favershams had not exaggerated—he was huge! Even Basil, taller than most mice, seemed small by comparison with this shaggy giant.

Suddenly he disappeared! We continued

running, and the mystery was soon made clear.

He had fallen down a deep crevasse. Cries of pain came to our ears. We anchored one end of our rope ladder in the hard snow, and carefully descended.

The poor creature had broken his wrist, which I set and splinted, and we helped him up the ladder.

He looked at us shyly out of his large brown eyes, and jabbered in some strange jargon.

Basil, an accomplished linguist, understood some of it, and made signs and gestures so that the two were soon communicating.

"He is grateful that we rescued him," Basil told me, "and will take us to his cave. He is friendly with the Tellmice, and visits them frequently, through a tunnel leading from his cave to the Lost Colony. We had better not fetch the others—this creature is too easily frightened, and may run away."

A full moon made the night as bright as day, and we followed the Snowmouse. An hour's climb brought us to his cave, high on the west face of Emmentaler. We had to stoop

to enter, but stood erect easily in the cave proper.

It was a large square room whose walls were covered with crude drawings of cave-mice. Basil went over every inch of the walls with his magnifying lens.

He flung himself down full length to peer at a drawing near the floor, and his eyes glittered.

"Bring another candle, Dawson. As I deduced, the Tellmice and Snowmice of long ago were friendly. For proof, here is a drawing signed by Byzant himself—the signature is unmistakable! And there are carved objects in this cave which no snowmouse ever made. I'll ask him to take us to the Lost Colony at once."

The Snowmouse agreed. Holding our candles high, we followed him down a narrow, winding tunnel, for a long time. Basil and I were tingling with excitement.

Then the walls of the tunnel were streaked with moonlight, and my heart sang within me! At long last we had reached the end of our search!

But I had rejoiced too soon! A rumbling noise came from within the mountain, and an enormous boulder tumbled down in front of us.

The tunnel was blocked!

"So near and yet so far," said Basil. "If we can turn it slightly, we may squeeze through."

We failed. The stone was far too heavy, and

the Snowmouse could not use his great strength because of his broken wrist.

Basil remarked wryly, "I fear I am guilty of a misstatement. In London I said I'd leave no stone unturned to find the Lost Colony. I said it again in Käsedorf. Yet here is one stone I *must* leave unturned!"

We went back to the cave. Our guide wept, for he thought he would never see his friends again.

Basil suggested to him that we might reach the Lost Colony from the top of the mountain.

The Snowmouse became terrified, and jabbered away at some length.

Basil translated. "He says there are evil spirits on the summit, that no one has ever

dared to go there, and that no one ever should. But you and I *will* go, Dawson, without the Snowmouse. We cannot let an old superstition swerve us from our goal!"

We slept in the cave that night. In the morning Basil gave the Snowmouse a note to take back to our camp. In it he instructed Tillary and the others to bring along a tentpole to be used as a lever for moving the stone.

The shaggy mouse, assured by Basil that all of us were friendly, left on his errand.

And then began the most momentous climb we had ever undertaken—the ascent to the summit!

Our progress, in the face of a stiff wind, was maddeningly slow. We plodded on, speaking little, for we knew we had to conserve our strength.

Emmentaler, and the icy blasts that threatened to make us lose our footing, seemed to be mocking us, challenging us to go on!

Still another ice fall loomed before us. Basil cut steps in it with his ax, but tired quickly in the high, thin air. He signaled, and I took

over. It was exhausting work, and it was soon
Basil's turn again.

But no sooner had he cut a dozen steps than
he cried, "*Voilá!* There's no more up! The
mountain is ours!"

Words cannot tell the joy of that historic
moment. We had made every mouse's dream
come true! We had conquered Mount Emmentaler!

We hoisted a small British flag, and also a
Swiss flag given us by the Mayor of Käsedorf.

Then, in a quaint mouse ceremony known
as the Mousegrave Ritual, we intertwined our

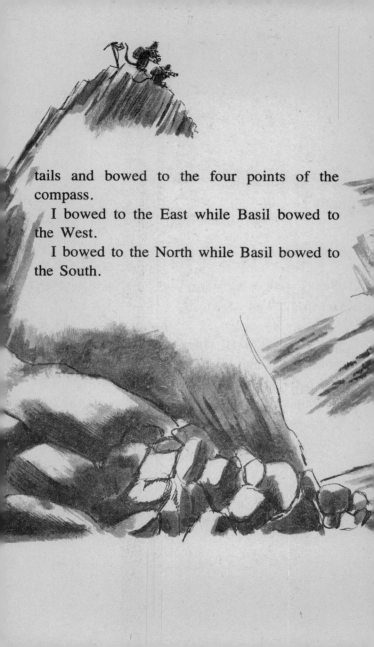

tails and bowed to the four points of the compass.

I bowed to the East while Basil bowed to the West.

I bowed to the North while Basil bowed to the South.

And then he said one word, "Observe!"
I turned around to see what was to be seen.
There, about a thousand feet below, lay a

valley, snugly nestled between two jutting cliffs!

Eagerly we whipped out our binoculars. We saw an old ruin of a castle, once built by humans. It had no roof, but the walls were still standing.

Within those walls we could see tiny huts ranged around a tiny village square, and signs of movement from the tiny beings who lived there.

Basil's voice was calm. "Shall we pay them a call?"

"Immediately, if not sooner!" I replied.

Never did two mice make a happier descent!

For the Lost Colony was no longer lost— Basil of Baker Street had found it!

14

The Valley of Missing Mice

Time had stood still in the Valley of Missing Mice.

Those who dwelt there lived just as their ancestors had lived, hundreds and hundreds of years ago. Seeing them clad in medieval dress was like opening a history book to pages far in the past.

They had observed our descent through spyglasses, and we were met by forty mice with bows and arrows. Once satisfied that we were friends, they welcomed us warmly, and showed us around the village built within the ruined, roofless castle.

The original Tellmice had been fortunate to find this castle, whose thick stone walls afforded the best possible shelter against the wild weather.

How picturesque everything seemed to our modern-day eyes—the quaint huts, the exquisite carvings, the colorful costumes of yesterday.

In the schoolyard stood an old wooden statue of the tyrant Heddmann. Each schoolmouse was required to shoot ten arrows each day at a wooden grape perched upon his head. As fast as a grape tumbled down, another ap-

peared, due to an ingenious mechanism concealed within Heddmann's head.

"Our youth is prepared to defend our freedom against all tyrants!" said Mayor Saanen.

"My dear Mayor, you are most wise," said Basil. "However, it is my happy duty to inform you that Switzerland regained her freedom six hundred years ago, in 1291. Many mouse expeditions tried to bring this news to your remote retreat, but none was able to find your Lost Colony."

100

The Mayor's eyes filled with tears of joy. Messengers summoned the Tellmice, a hundred strong.

When they were assembled Basil said, "I bring news to gladden your hearts. Patriots, your beloved land is as free and as independent as the United States of America!"

We saw blank bewilderment on their faces.

The schoolmaster stepped forward. "What is this United States of America? Never have I heard of it!"

Now we knew why they were puzzled—the Tellmice had been cut off from the world for six centuries!

There was much history to impart to them, and we tackled the task, taking turns in the telling.

The Tellmice listened closely, not missing a syllable.

We spoke of the Age of Discovery—of the English, French, and Spanish explorers, of the American Revolution, of all the European conflicts.

It saddened us to list the many wars that had been waged, but we were proud to tell of the great strides made in science and art and music and literature.

Imagine—they had never heard of Shakespeare, or Beethoven, or Michaelangelo, or Pasteur, or Walt Whitman, or Sherlock Holmes!

We described steamboats, submarines, locomotives, wireless. Their eyes opened wide with wonder!

When told about telephones, the Mayor said, "Would it be possible to yodel into this instrument?"

"Most assuredly!" said Basil. "And you shall all do so when you accompany us back to Käsedorf."

We learned that no Tellmouse had ever gone to the summit of Emmentaler. The Mayor explained.

"The original Tellmice feared that Heddmann's mice might see them, and that they would be brought back to the tyrant's prison. They passed a law forbidding any mouse to go outside the castle walls, a law still kept."

Basil and I thumped each other heartily on

the back. We *had* been the first mice to conquer the mountain!

Before dark the Snowmouse and Tillary and the others arrived, having managed to move the stone.

The villagers welcomed the giant warmly. They believed him to be the last of the Adorable Snowmice.

Upon hearing this, Lord Adrian said, ''Tell him I saw another Snowmouse in camp last

night—smaller, and far more graceful. Perhaps he can find her."

Delighted and excited, the Snowmouse hugged Lord Adrian and ran off. This was the last we saw of the shaggy mouse. It is to be hoped that he and his mate are now raising a family of "adorable" little ones.

Next day we climbed to the summit, that all might taste the thrill of going to the top of Emmentaler.

Halfway down, we were able to repay the St. Bernard for his many kindnesses. We came upon two human children, fast asleep in the snow!

Basil acted promptly. "Tellmice, aim your arrows at their legs! The children will freeze unless they awaken and move about. The arrows will feel like pinpricks to these huge creatures, but will succeed in waking them up! The rest of us will yodel for Elmo!"

Our loud yodels soon fetched the St. Bernard.

"Thank you, Basil, with all my heart. I was sent out to find these lost ones, and you have helped me."

"Think nothing of it," replied Basil. "*Noblesse oblige!* I am honored to call so kind and greathearted a dog my friend. 'Till we meet again!'"

15
Hail to the Hero!

We returned to Käsedorf on the holiday that marked six hundred years of Swiss freedom—August 2, 1891.

Flags flew! Bells rang! Bands played! Children strewed posies in our path, and the beauteous Relda herself hung a garland of flowers about Basil's neck and kissed him on both cheeks.

The villagers had gay wreaths for all the Tellmice, and all the expeditioneers. The

Mayor presented Basil with a gold medal and praised us to the skies.

Basil told newspapermice from near and far how he had solved the age-old mystery, and the tiny town of Käsedorf became world-famous, just as he had promised.

Expeditioneers and Tellmice then toured Switzerland. Admiring mice thronged around us wherever we appeared.

The mice of Zirl took us through a catgut factory, owned by people. There Basil gathered enough scraps to string his violin for years.

In Zurich we made a night visit to a watch factory, also owned by people. The watch-works were wonderful, but we had to watch out for the watchman!

In Zermatt we went through the National Mousetrap Museum, and learned lifesaving lore, for the lecturers explained exactly how each trap worked.

We were sorry we could not visit Zyzzzz, the Swiss mouse capital. Zyzzzz was besieged by bumblebees.

Soon it was time for the expedition to disband. Parting was sad, but we would all be friends forever. The Tellmice had decided to make their castle a skiing resort, and said we would always be welcome.

At last Basil and I crossed the English Channel. Six Tellmice accompanied us, for the Mousmopolitan scientists and historians wished to learn all there was to know about the Lost Colony, past and present.

That evening the Museum gave a banquet for Basil. Hundreds of mice in the arts and sciences attended. He was elected to lifetime membership in the Royal Academy of Mousology and presented with the highest honor of all—the Award of the Cat's Eye!

Accepting the prized emerald charm, he said, "I have studied our own paws, and those of the Adorable Snowmouse, who is a throwback to primitive cavemice. My findings will startle and delight you. I deduce that at some distant date mice may develop thumbs!"

The audience cheered for five full minutes!

Basil continued, "Some day mice and men may work hand in paw to attain greatness. Will it be in the conquest of space? One can

only wonder. I predict that man will begin unlocking the secrets of space in about 1960. Then mice and men alike may taste the fruits of victory—or should I say the crumbs?"

The mighty thunder of applause reached the ears of an alley cat. We snuffed out the candles, and cowered in the darkness until the monster had gone.

Later, the master detective and I sat half-sleeping before the fire in Baker Street, Number 221,B.

We were two tired mice. The case had left

Basil thin and gaunt, much in need of a holiday.

There was a tapping at the window. Basil opened it, to reveal the beady eyes of Cyril the Stoolpigeon.

"Congratulations, Guv'n'r! Sherlock 'Olmes would be proud of ye! I brought a message, free! A little Oriental bird told me that Ratigan sailed for the kingdom of Bengistan to make trouble for the Maharajah."

Basil thanked him, and shut the window. He straightened to his full height, his eyes alert and wide-awake.

"The Professor is as clever as ever," he remarked. "He knew this news would send me hightailing it off to the Orient. This time he'll not slip through my paws!"

I groaned aloud. "Am I to understand that tomorrow we pack again, so soon after unpacking?"

"Precisely," said Basil. "Meanwhile, the hour is late, old friend—we'd best be off to bed. And may our dreams be safe from tabbies and toms!"

About the Author and Illustrator

EVE TITUS is the author of twenty children's books, including those about the French cheese-tasting mouse, Anatole. A professional concert pianist, she has always had two loves—writing and music. Miss Titus originated and personally conducts her Storybook Writing Seminar several times a year, and during the summer in Europe as a traveling workshop combined with a children's literature program. Because of Mouse Basil, Miss Titus is President of the Sherlock Holmes Society of Los Angeles. Born and raised in New York City, she lived in Mexico for three years. California is her present home, and summers are spent on a small Greek island, writing and giving her workshop. Of the first *Basil of Baker Street* mystery, Adrian M. Conan Doyle wrote the author, "May I offer you my heart-felt congratulations. It is a simply wonderful creation, and I can assure you that my father would have revelled in every page." Numerous Sherlockian collectors prize the *Basil of Baker Street* mysteries, which include *Basil of Baker Street, Basil and the Pygmy Cats,* and *Basil in Mexico,* available in Archway Paperback editions.

PAUL GALDONE came to this country from Budapest, Hungary, and studied at the Art Students League in New York. He is a well-known illustrator of children's literature and lives with his wife and their two children in Rockland County, New York.